The Plate

Written by
Julia Wall

Illustrated by
Marjorie Scott

We went to see Grandpa.
We went in our old car.

Grandpa had lots of plates
on his walls.
Grandpa had a plate he really liked.
It was at the bottom of his stairs.
It was a yellow plate with a ship on it.

My sister had a ball.
I was at the top of the stairs.

My sister was at the bottom
of the stairs near the yellow plate.
My sister threw the ball to me.
I threw the ball back to my sister.

Mum came in.
"Do not throw that ball inside,"
said Mum.
"You will break something."

"Yes, Mum, " we said.

When Mum went out,
my sister threw the ball to me.
I threw it back to my sister.

My sister did not catch the ball.
The ball hit the yellow plate
with the ship on it.
The yellow plate fell down.

Mum and Grandpa came running in. "I told you not to throw that ball inside!" said Mum.

Grandpa looked at his plate.
He looked sad.

"We are sorry, Grandpa," we said.

"Do not feel bad," said Grandpa.
"I can fix my plate
with some glue."

Mum was angry.
We drove home in our old car.

13

When we went to see Grandpa again,
the yellow plate with the ship on it
was back on the wall.
We could only see the cracks
where Grandpa had fixed it
if we looked closely.

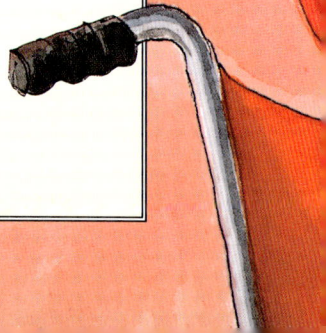